Top Fin

Dolphin Dives

by Addie Meyer Sanders

This book is dedicated with joy to Buddy, Matthew, Wesley, Kodie, Kailyn, Thomas, and you, the reader. I'd like to thank . . . Dr. David Nathanson in Florida who so readily shared his wonderful Dolphin Human Therapy Program with me. The Dolphin Research Center where I enjoyed my swim. The East End Children's Book Writers and Illustrators group who patiently listened to my dolphin tales. My faithful, supportive family and friends. Elizabeth Castelli, my super 8th-grade student editor. Mary Bush, a writer's dream editor. Kristin, David, and Karrin who were always ready to hear more. Dave for his encouragement and wonderful love. God who makes all things possible.

About the Author

Addie Meyer Sanders grew up on a canal in Baldwin Harbor on Long Island. She has lived on or near water for most of her life. That encouraged her love of clamming, crabbing, boating, swimming, and doing water aerobics. She also enjoyed swimming with dolphins, which she did as research for this book.

With a teaching certificate and master's degree in secondary education, Ms. Sanders has been a teacher, a writer, and a poet-in-residence. She continues to visit schools and conduct writing workshops with children.

Ms. Sanders met her husband in high school. They have three children, Kristin, David Jr., and Karrin, as well as six grandchildren.

Cover & Inside Illustration: Margo Bock

Contents

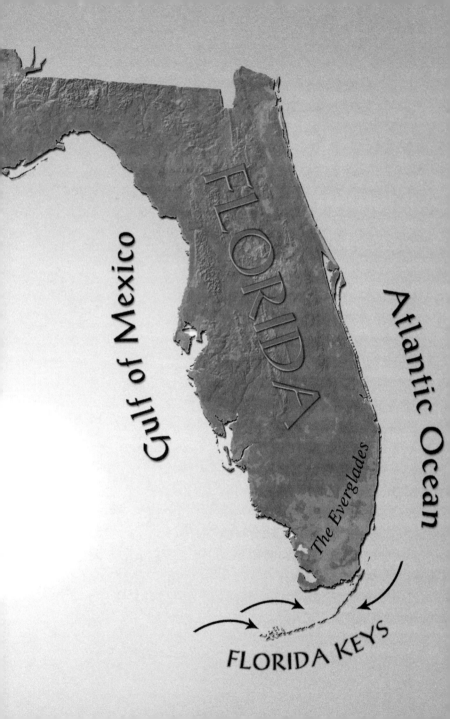

Prologue:
Kove Key

Kelly sat curled up in the school bus. Her arms circled her legs. Her knuckles were white from clenching her hands for over an hour. Kelly pressed her forehead against the window. She watched steamy south Florida pass under her frozen gaze.

For miles, the Everglades blurred behind her. The River of Grass, a giant saltwater marsh, looked like a huge green field. Songbirds called through the reeds.

Just the thought of the wildlife and alligators hiding in the salty water raised goose bumps on Kelly's flesh. A white egret flew along with the bus. A bald eagle watched from on top of a telephone pole.

Soon Kelly felt the air change. Cooler air entered the bus. The bus was traveling along the thin strip of highway that separated endless turquoise waters. The Atlantic Ocean was on the left. The Gulf of Mexico was on the right. Kelly welcomed the salty air.

PROLOGUE

She had never been to the keys. She'd only lived in Florida for three years. But now, just before her fourteenth birthday and the start of high school next fall, she had been assigned to Dolphin Dives.

Questions flashed through her head like the huge billboards that lined the overseas highway in Key Largo. Why me? Why now?

Okay, so she hadn't spoken in three years—ever since the accident. And her mother and teachers were hoping this would help. But how? Kelly wondered.

In three years, she had perfected the art of being invisible. But how would she stay hidden with only five kids in the program?

The bright reds and blues of popular restaurants whizzed by. Diving-gear shops dotted the road. Divers loved the keys' coral reefs.

An open shark's mouth marked the entrance to the tourist center. Kelly grimaced as she read the sign— *Best Green Turtle Soup.*

Kelly closed her eyes and leaned back in the seat. She pictured a map of the keys in her head. They were getting close. Kove Key was about a quarter of the way down the 110-mile road that connected dozens of keys like polished pearls on a string.

Kelly knew that Kove Key looked like a backwards K. Highway 1 cut down the side of the ocean. The fork of the K formed a protected cove on the gulf side. That cove harbored Dolphin Dives.

Kelly thought about the other three kids on the bus. She knew their names, even though she didn't *know* them. A couple had been in her classes. But they hadn't spoken to her. Of course, she hadn't spoken with anyone.

Today, no one spoke. Were they sleeping? she wondered. Or were they nervous too?

Kelly unclasped her hands and stretched her legs. They passed a large sign—WELCOME TO KOVE KEY. The bus turned onto a narrow road.

Overgrown jade mangrove bushes scraped along the sides of the bus. Kelly's stomach lurched. They were getting closer.

The bus turned again. Pastel houses lined the sandy street. Then she saw the sign—DEAD END. NO EXIT.

Kelly trembled. That was how she felt. There was no way to escape now.

The bus stopped. The doors opened with a swoosh. A pale yellow house surrounded by a high fence loomed in front of them.

Kelly took a deep breath as she stepped off the bus. Her face was as pale as the white sand under her feet. She walked slowly toward the gate.

Jumping In

The dolphin jumped high in the air. Her huge, long, perfectly muscled silver body glistened in the late afternoon sun. Rainbow sprays filled the air. She flipped and landed on her side. That sent a monster wave crashing over the dock. It soaked the kids.

Shaking, Kelly inched along the fence. She tried to keep her balance on the slippery stones. Kelly's green eyes searched the water.

Will the dolphin jump again? she wondered. Half of her wanted it to, and half was afraid that it would. A shiver rippled down her spine. Her heart raced.

She pressed her back and hands against the rough fence. Splinters pierced her palms. She backed away from the giant dolphin.

"Hey, mon, that's one huge hunk of meat!" gasped Palo. His eyes swung between the gate and the water. Dozens of shiny black braids whipped around his head. They were almost the same color as his skin.

"Yo, mon, I'm out of here!" he said.

Kelly agreed with Palo. But her eyes kept returning to the water. Floating docks dotted the surface. Foot-high mesh fences divided the water into areas as big as football fields.

A lot of good those fences do, Kelly thought. She remembered the high leap that had greeted them.

Kelly wanted to scream, "Get me out of here!" But, as usual, she felt an imaginary hand gripping her throat. It was the hand that stopped sounds. At the same time, there was another hand on her back trying to push the words out.

Kelly had fought this battle every day since the accident. But today, panic rose inside her like the dolphin rising out of the sea.

Suddenly, a loud whiny voice made Kelly jump. "Look at me! Just *look* at me! I'm soaked! My chair's soaked! I'm leaving. Now!" Betsy screeched.

Kelly had seen Betsy on the bus. What was *she* doing here? Kelly wondered.

Struggling, Betsy pushed her wheelchair down the path. Kelly froze. She wanted to help, but it could mean a confrontation. She couldn't risk that.

Betsy grumbled, "Why can't this place have cement walks? I could tip over on these stones."

Betsy pushed herself to the picnic table. A palm-leaf umbrella provided shade. But Betsy didn't cool down.

"This is dumb. I shouldn't be here," she grumbled.

Palo moved quickly to help Betsy. Kelly felt better. She was glad Palo was there.

Kelly had always thought that Palo seemed fun. He was always joking around at school. And he always seemed happy—even when he was getting into trouble for his clowning around. Teachers were constantly telling Palo to sit still and be quiet.

"Here, this'll cool you down," he joked. He eased Betsy deeper into the shade. "Your chair won't rust. But maybe it will sink," he laughed.

Kelly watched. If looks could kill, Palo would be gone. But Betsy chose not to reply. She smoothed her chin-length brown hair. Satisfied, Betsy sat taller.

Kelly read Betsy's body language. It said, *I'll never be back*. Kelly didn't blame her. Being here in a wheelchair had to be doubly scary.

Kelly scanned the water. It ran dark and deep. It was steel blue speckled with silver sunlight.

Black fins sliced through the surface. Dolphins? She remembered the giant eye. Work with them? No way!

Kelly suddenly realized she was standing alone. She moved to the table and sat down. Kelly twisted a long auburn curl around her finger and chewed on the end.

BOOM! Kelly bounced. Palo crashed onto her bench.

"Hey, mon, you gonna protect me?" Palo asked, throwing his arm around Kelly. His braids danced on her shoulder. Kelly trembled.

"Hey," he said, popping his hand up as if he had touched a hot stove. "You're shaking! A lot of help you'll be."

Kelly forced a smile. But inside, she decided they were in trouble if even Palo was scared. Usually, he'd try anything.

WHAM! Heads turned as the gate crashed open.

"Here!" shouted an angry teen. He shoved a kid through the gate. The boy fell on the stones, scraping his knees. He quickly pushed himself up and angrily swiped at the blood on his legs.

The older boy's words hit like fists, "If you ever miss that bus again and I have to drive you here, you're dead! You hear me, little brother?"

The tall boy turned on the heel of his heavy black boot and disappeared. The gate slammed behind him.

The bleeding kid kicked stones at the gate. A sharp *ping ping* filled the air.

Kelly couldn't believe her eyes. They were brothers? She'd always wanted a brother or sister. But she'd never dreamed one could be so mean. How awful for Jake!

Finally, Palo spoke. "Uh, hi, Jake. Do you want to sit?" Palo stood, offering his spot.

Kelly worried that Jake would sit next to her. But Jake's face turned crimson. His unruly dark curls hid even darker eyes. His fists tightened.

Kelly held her breath. But Jake didn't sit.

Instead, he growled at Palo, "Shut up!"

Jake's head sank into his shoulders. He kicked more stones. Kelly watched his angry eyes and his balled fists. He was looking for a fight. But then, seeing that he didn't have any takers, he whirled around and punched the fence.

Kelly's heart raced. She didn't like confrontation. And she was trapped between Jake and the sea. Her breath caught in her throat.

Then she remembered the article from the teen magazine she'd read. It had said, "When you're in a tight spot and you find it hard to breathe, think these words as you slowly inhale and exhale. In. Out. In. Out."

Kelly tried it. She began to relax. In. Out. I can't pass out. In. Out . . .

2

Splash

"Hey, what are you doing so close to the water?" a tanned blond girl shouted. She suddenly appeared from inside the house. "Move away. Now!"

Kelly saw that the blond was yelling at Tyler. She hadn't noticed the school's track star move closer to the water. Kelly wondered what Mr. Perfect was doing here.

She could guess why she and the others were here. She didn't speak. Palo was always goofing around. Jake was always fighting. And Betsy hated everything. But why Tyler? And how could the dolphins help any of them?

Tyler's voice shook the air. "Are you in charge here?" he demanded.

"Yes, I'm the trainer. I'll be working with your group," she said, nervously eyeing the kids. Hostile stares glared back at her. "I'm Sue," she added.

Then Sue welcomed each of them by name. It was clear that she knew a little about the members of her small group.

Kelly watched Sue's lip quiver and her eyelids flutter. Kelly read her body language. Sue was anxious too.

Tyler said, "Well, it doesn't look like you want to be here any more than we do. So why are we?"

"Right!" Betsy added. "This is a mistake! You can see why. I'm in a wheelchair. I must be taken home immediately!"

Kelly listened to Betsy's words. Betsy was overly dramatic. But, in this case, Kelly agreed with her.

Sue stood without speaking. Kelly watched her. I'd like to look like Sue, she thought.

Sue was pretty and athletic. And she was probably a great swimmer, Kelly reasoned.

Kelly pushed unruly reddish brown curls behind her ears. Sue's hair swung in golden sheets. Kelly squinted at Sue's face. She couldn't find a freckle anywhere. Kelly touched her own connect-the-dot face. Great, Kelly thought miserably. Sue was a cover girl!

Finally, Sue planted her hands on her hips and said, "Nobody's leaving until the bus returns. So relax. And you're right, I'm nervous. I'm not sure what your school wants. All I know is that most kids love the dolphins. We'll work it out."

"Are you trying to convince us or yourself?" Tyler mumbled.

Sue ignored Tyler. She flipped her hair forward. It formed a curtain between her and the kids. Then Sue clasped it back into a ponytail. She was ready.

Sue put a hand on Betsy's shoulder, "Hey, you guys, it'll be okay. You look scared to death."

"I'm not scared," Jake spat out. He kicked a shower of stones into the water.

"Hey, none of that!" Sue shouted. She lurched toward Jake.

"Don't touch me!" Jake hissed.

Sue stopped short but warned, "Don't you do anything to jeopardize the dolphins. Stones could cut the dolphins' skin or eyes. It could cause infections or even death."

Jake stared. He folded his arms. *Don't tell me what to do!* his look screamed.

Sue inhaled deeply and forced a smile. "Hey, kids," she said. "We're going to be together for six weeks. Let's make the best of it. Okay?"

Palo jumped up. "Yeah, cool, mon! I'll hop in with the dolphins. That's why we're here, right? How about it?" Palo asked, tripping to the water. He put the palms of his hands together over his head, ready for a clown dive.

"Whoa," Sue called. She caught Palo by the edge of his shirt. Sue led Palo back to the table. "How about some orientation first."

"Wait!" Betsy yelled. "Do you actually think we're going to go in the water with those . . . those *giants*? We could be killed! They weigh hundreds of pounds!"

"You're right," Sue said. "Dolphins can weigh up to 700 pounds. But they won't hurt you. They're also very smart."

"And beautiful," Betsy admitted. "But they have their world, and I have mine. Dolphins don't come to class with me. So why should I be in a class with them?"

Even in the hot Florida sun, Kelly shivered. Was this true? They had to *swim* with the dolphins? Was that why the school had sent them here?

Sue answered Betsy. "No one has to go in the water unless they want to. And our dolphins haven't eaten anyone." Sue grinned. "At least, not yet!"

"Everyone's a comedian," Palo said.

"That's it. I'm out of here. Now!" Betsy ordered, pushing away from the table.

Everyone ignored Betsy. They knew she couldn't go anywhere without the bus.

Then Tyler spoke. "So why are we here?" His deep voice echoed off the water.

My thoughts exactly, Kelly thought. She let her eyes fall on Tyler—tall, terrific Tyler. Short, sun-bleached hair crowned his head, his eyebrows, and even his arms. Something about him made her heart flip.

They'd had math together last year. But she was sure he didn't know her. After all, he was a star, and she was invisible.

Kelly wondered what it would be like to be so sure of yourself. To know what you wanted and then work for it. But Kelly didn't know what she wanted. She changed her mind faster than she could flip TV channels. And her grades were up and down—just like her moods.

Guilt and sadness surfaced whenever she did feel happy. But that wasn't very often anyway. Most of the time, Kelly didn't know how to feel—or how to act.

Kelly remembered when she had lost her speech. It had been after the accident. That's when she had learned that her words could hurt—even kill. So she learned not to speak. She couldn't risk hurting someone else.

Daydreaming, Kelly twisted a curl and chewed on it. Finally, Sue's voice scattered Kelly's thoughts.

"Your high school decided to try Dolphin Dives. You were selected to be the first in the program."

"Well, aren't we the lucky ones," Betsy sniffed sarcastically.

Sue rolled her eyes. "They even thought you might enjoy it."

"Well, they were wrong!" Betsy snapped.

"Maybe. Maybe not," Sue said. "But we won't know until we try."

"Try! Ha! Do you think I'm going in the water with those monsters? Do you know how I landed in a wheelchair? Diving. You can lead a kid to water, but you can't make her swim!"

"Shut up, Betsy!" Jake commanded. "We'll put in our time today. And then we'll split."

"Nope," Sue said. "No one's leaving. We're together for six Mondays. But you won't have to do anything you don't want to."

"Great," Tyler complained. "A complete waste of time. We have to drive to the keys, spend time here, and then drive back. A whole afternoon shot for six weeks. I could be training."

"For what? The Olympics? Like you're gonna get there," Jake sneered. He still wanted to fight.

"I think Tyler's going to the Olympics," Palo said, jumping up. "He's fast. Mon, when I run, my legs twist like pretzels." Palo ran, twisting his legs and falling.

Kelly admired how Palo stood up for Tyler. Maybe if she had, he'd know she was alive. But right now, she had bigger problems—like how she was going to deal with the dolphins.

Then the sea separated as a dolphin rose high in the air. The shadow dwarfed the group. The dolphin flipped and splashed down. Water sprayed over the dock, covering it like a wet blanket. Tension as real as the splash filled the air.

"What a jump! Does that dolphin have a name?" Palo asked quietly.

"Sure," Sue said. "Would you believe it's Splash?"

Palo laughed out loud. "Hey, it suits him."

"Splash is a female," Sue corrected. "She's a beautiful 500-pound female."

Hearing her name, Splash popped up. Enormous eyes searched the shore. They found Kelly. Splash and Kelly connected. A strange peace filled Kelly.

Splash went under again. Then her whole body rose out of the water. She walked backward on her tail, nodding her head toward the kids.

"Hey, look. She's inviting us in," Palo said.

Splash's mouth opened in a wide grin. Friendly whistles and clicks filled the air.

"She's laughing at us," Betsy snarled.

But Kelly knew that Splash wasn't making fun of them. She and Splash had communicated. She still couldn't imagine getting in the water with her, though.

Then Kelly watched a steel gray fin break the surface and cut a path through the water. Would the dolphins help her overcome her fears? Or would they add more?

Kelly shivered. She wrapped her arms around her knees, holding them tightly to her chest. Even though she felt peace from Splash, she couldn't stop shaking. Breathe, she told herself. In. Out.

3

Gearing Up

Kelly watched Sue carry out a large black mesh bag from the storage shed. Sue emptied brightly colored rubber masks, snorkels, and flippers onto the table. Kelly stared at the equipment needed to enter the dolphins' world.

Jake's fist pounded the table. The group and the equipment jumped. "What's this junk?" he demanded, claiming Palo's bench. Palo slid next to Tyler.

Sue spread out the gear. "Want to see what fits? Now that you've had the official welcome from Splash," Sue persisted, "you can try these on."

The only response was from Splash. She recognized her name and popped up. Her bright eyes and natural smile took in the group. Happy squeals filled the air.

"Look," called Palo, "her mouth is open. She's saying, 'Palo, come swim with me.' "

Kelly smiled. Palo always made her smile.

Sue laughed. "You're right, Palo. Splash is talking. But dolphins open their mouths to mimic us. Dolphin sounds really come from the blowholes on the tops of their heads."

"No way. I've never heard that. And I even read a book about dolphins once," Betsy said.

"Books don't know anything," Jake grumbled.

Trying to keep peace, Sue said, "You're both right. You can learn from books, but there are other ways to learn as well. Sometimes you have to take a risk and jump in."

Jake grunted. Kelly knew Jake was street-smart. She was sure he had to "jump in" often.

Kelly noticed the jagged scar on his cheek. A knife wound? What was his life like? she wondered. She suspected his life was full of trouble—even at home. Jake probably had reasons to be angry.

Kelly forced her mind back to Sue. Sue couldn't really want them to swim with the dolphins.

Tyler blurted out, "Are we going in the water with Splash?"

Kelly straightened. Again Tyler had asked what she was thinking.

"Some of you may," Sue said. "It's up to you. It takes courage. But it will be worth it."

"Cool," Palo said, jumping up. "I'm ready."

"Hold it, Palo," Sue said. "Not yet. Your enthusiasm is great, but first you have to listen. It's important to your safety and the safety of the dolphins."

Kelly looked around. Palo squatted on the edge of the bench. Tyler folded his arms across his chest. Betsy's eyes darted anxiously to the water. Jake's hands formed fists.

Everyone was quiet for a moment. A salty breeze circled them. For the first time, Kelly saw them as a group.

Seeing she had everyone's attention, Sue continued. "Remember, you don't have to go in the water until you're ready. And I'll go in with you if you want."

Betsy erupted, "You don't get it! I'll never go in that water. In case you haven't noticed, I'm in a wheelchair. Diving is how I got here."

Betsy glared at the group. No one spoke.

"It's not like I'm scared," she went on. "I'm just not going."

Kelly watched as Betsy's bravery dissolved. Sudden tears flooded Betsy's eyes. She turned to Sue. "There are things I can't do. And that," she said, shaking a finger at the water, "is one of them."

Sue twisted her ponytail into a bun. "I'll bet there are things you can do that you haven't thought of. We have an aqua seat for people who use wheelchairs. They love to feel the dolphins and meet them face-to-face. They say dolphins accept them just as they are."

"Yeah, right," Betsy mumbled. But her eyes glanced over the water. Kelly also looked for the aqua seat.

"So, Sue," Tyler asked, "how do we know if this stuff fits?" He fingered the gear.

Jake shifted on the bench. He sat on his hands and looked away. He wasn't getting sucked into this.

"I know what these are," Palo said. He picked up a pair of black rubber flippers. "Duck feet!" Palo threw his foot on the table and tried pulling the webbed flipper over his foot.

"Flippers," Sue corrected. "But, Palo, your feet are too big for those. You need your size."

"Big feet? Are you saying I have big feet?" Palo joked. "Here, I'll shorten them." Grabbing his ankle, he twisted his leg and stuffed his toes into his mouth.

"Gross!" Betsy sputtered. She glanced at her still legs. "How did you *do* that? You're a human pretzel."

Kelly smiled. Palo really could be a comedian. A lot of comics got started by entertaining their classmates. And Palo could definitely make people laugh.

Sue continued explaining. "The flippers will help you move in the water. The mask will help you see. Just adjust the straps on the mask. It goes over your eyes and nose. Place it on your face and breathe in. If it stays, then you have a good fit, and water won't leak in."

Palo tried on the mask and said, "Hey, look! A window!"

"You need to spit in it," Sue told Palo. "Then wipe the spit around the plastic so it won't fog up."

"Spit in it? That's disgusting!" Betsy choked. "I don't use stuff people spit in."

Sue laughed. "They've all been disinfected. So there are no germs."

"But if it's over your nose, how do you breathe?" Palo asked, examining the mask.

"Take this," Jake said. He shoved a snorkel at Palo. "Shove it in your mouth."

Palo took the snorkel and stuck it in his mouth. Then he found flippers that fit and stood up.

"I'm ready," he choked. Suddenly, he lost his balance. He tumbled head over flippers onto the stones. They scattered beneath him.

Palo crashed near Betsy. She laughed, "You look like a sea monster."

"Good flip, Palo," Tyler said. "But I think Splash has you beat."

Kelly grinned. Maybe this would be okay. This group could be fun. And she had been lonely these last few years.

Maybe she'd even get brave and go near the water. She'd like to feel a dolphin.

Sue smiled. "Well, Palo, thanks for showing us how not to use the equipment. Now, I'll show you the proper way. I'll need a helper. Kelly, come here please."

Kelly's eyes widened. Her heart sank like a stone tossed into the sea. Doesn't Sue know I'm invisible?

Not me, Kelly's eyes pleaded. But Sue gently took her hand. Kelly stood. She moved like she was walking in cement.

All eyes were on her. She wanted to run. But there was no place to go. This must be a nightmare! Her mind was racing, but her body barely moved.

Her breath came in gasps. Breathe, she thought. Then she felt a warm, supporting hand on her back.

4

Bridges

"Here, I'll help," Tyler said. He reached around to adjust the strap on Kelly's mask. Kelly blinked. She knew she had bug eyes through the plastic window.

She was standing in front of the whole group. And Tyler was helping her. Shivers rippled through her body. She wasn't invisible anymore. Would she survive?

Sue watched. "Thank you, Tyler. It's snug. Now water can't get in. But it has to be comfortable too."

She looked in the window covering Kelly's face. "Is it comfortable?" Sue asked.

Comfortable? Kelly's eyes glistened like green pools. She felt ready to pass out. And Sue asked if she was *comfortable*! But Kelly wanted to please. So she nodded in agreement.

"The snorkel goes in your mouth. Bite down on it," Sue instructed.

"Yuck," Betsy groaned. "How many people have chewed on that?"

"Don't worry, Betsy," Sue answered. "They're all sanitized. No germs allowed."

"Yuck! Germs," Palo said. He screwed up his face as if he were eating lemons.

By now, Sue was getting used to Palo. So she ignored him and went on explaining. "The tube gets tucked under the mask's strap. Then when you swim, you continue to breathe."

"Good plan," Tyler said, fitting Kelly's snorkel under the strap. Kelly didn't move.

"Try these flippers, Kelly," Sue said.

Kelly sat and tried on the flippers. They fit. But Kelly didn't stand up. She feared that she'd fly flippers over face as Palo had.

"Good, Kelly," Sue said. "Now everyone try on gear. Find out what fits. Then check the numbers on your equipment. Remember your numbers for next week."

Tyler grabbed gear to try. But Jake just stood there. He locked his arms tightly and glared.

Betsy's hands were red from gripping her chair. Muttering, she repeated Sue's words, "*Next* week. Not me. I won't be here."

Kelly heard Betsy's comments. Pulling off her mask, Kelly listened for other arguments. But no one else seemed to be paying attention to Betsy.

And, no one is paying attention to me, either, Kelly noticed. She breathed in slowly, beginning to calm down.

Sue moved throughout the group. She adjusted gear wherever necessary.

"Can you breathe?" Sue asked Palo. He nodded.

Sue laughed, "Well, I've found a way to shut you up. Snorkels for everyone."

"But that won't always work," Palo's voice gurgled around the snorkel.

"I can't wear flippers," Betsy whined, shoving the gear aside. "They'd be weights on my feet. I'd drown."

"Sometimes we surprise ourselves by doing things we thought we couldn't do." Sue tried for lightness. "And besides, we haven't lost anyone . . ."

"At least, not yet," Tyler moaned, repeating the joke.

"You guys catch on fast," Sue said. "And you're right, Betsy. You don't have to wear flippers. We have water socks for you. They're lighter. Another diver, Amy, has cerebral palsy. She uses the water socks too."

Kelly watched Betsy digest this information. Then she looked at the water. Tall fins crisscrossed the surface into tic-tac-toe squares.

Suddenly, Betsy looked a little more positive. If a girl with cerebral palsy could swim with the dolphins, maybe she could too.

"So will these sock things protect me from the dolphins?" Betsy asked.

"Actually, Betsy," Sue explained, "the socks protect the dolphins."

"Yeah, right. *If* I decide to go in the water with those creatures, they're going to need protection from *me*? I don't think so!" Betsy said.

Kelly wondered about that too. But she would never have said so. Kelly had never been much of a talker—even before. She had always been afraid that kids would laugh at her. She admired Betsy for saying how she felt.

Sue explained, "If your legs and feet are just floating in the water, a sharp toenail could scratch a dolphin's skin or eye. Infection could set in. That could mean death. Dolphins don't have immunity to germs that we carry. So socks and flippers protect the dolphins from us."

"Well, that's great for the dolphins," Betsy persisted. "But who'll protect *me* from the dolphins?"

As if on cue, two dolphins jumped toward each other. They passed each other in a graceful arc. Glittering water droplets trailed behind them.

"Hey, they're making a bridge!" Palo shouted.

Everyone's eyes flew to the water.

"Look, rainbows," Betsy cried, seeing the colorful sprays. Sensing they had center stage, the dolphins jumped again. They squealed and whistled.

Kelly trembled. They were beautiful. But they sure were big. Fear seized her. Then she thought about Sue's words to Betsy. Could I swim with the dolphins even though I don't feel like I can? Kelly wondered.

Kelly remembered something she'd read once. *Courage is being afraid and trying anyway.* Could she try?

The water held secrets—and fears of the unknown. But the dolphins jumped free. Would she be free from her fears in the water? Or would her secrets drag her down?

Kelly jumped. The honk of the school bus had interrupted her thoughts. Quickly, the group removed the diving gear and tossed it back onto the table.

"Gotta go," Jake growled. "Too bad. Looks like we're out of time," he added sarcastically.

Betsy nodded in agreement. She pushed herself through the gate.

"Don't forget the numbers on your equipment," Sue called as the group raced to the bus. "Then we can get started right away next week."

"Not me!" Jake shouted. "I'm not coming back."

"She'll never see me again!" Betsy snapped. She wheeled herself toward the bus.

Kelly packed the gear into the black mesh bag. Maybe I'll hit the library and pick out some books about dolphins, she thought.

"I'll be back," Palo said. "I want to swim with Splash. Splash, where are you?"

Hearing her name, Splash popped up and nodded.

"See! There she is. She wants me," Palo told Sue.

"Yeah, she wants you for dinner," Tyler said. He grabbed Palo's arm and dragged him toward the bus. "Come on. Quit stalling. I have to get back. I have to run today."

Kelly entered the bus. She slid into the seat behind the driver. Resting her head, she stared out the window.

Soon they were speeding along Highway 1 again. Palm trees whizzed by in a green feathery blur.

The John Pennekamp Coral Reef State Park appeared on Kelly's right. Clear blue-green seas invited divers to explore the still waters. White long-necked cranes dotted the grassy marshes. A red-tailed hawk hunted in tight circles above the bus.

Salty hot air poured in through open windows. Kelly wondered if they'd be back. She wasn't sure whether she wanted to return or not. She was scared of swimming with those giant fins and powerful tails. And yet, somehow, the dolphins called to her.

Kelly closed her eyes. Would Tyler be back? Would he help her again?

What about Jake? He'd probably pick a fight and get expelled just to stay away. But could kids get expelled in the summer?

She knew Palo would return. He was the only one who seemed sure about swimming with the dolphins.

And what about poor Betsy? It must be hard for her to be around water, Kelly thought.

Then Kelly worried about herself. If she went into the water, how would it change her? She remembered Splash's eyes—the contact they had seemed to make with hers.

Something inside her stirred. A tiny burst of hope warmed Kelly. Maybe the dolphins could somehow help her find her voice.

5

No Way Out

Kelly yawned and rubbed her tired eyes. She hadn't slept well again last night. In fact, she hadn't slept well ever since she had gotten the letter from school. Why did she have to meet with the principal?

Well, she'd find out soon, Kelly thought. The meeting was today. Kelly recalled the letter's words.

All students involved in the Dolphin Dives program will meet with Mr. Garcia at 10 a.m. on Wednesday.

Kelly looked in the mirror. Dark circles hung beneath her eyes. I can't go looking like this, she thought.

But she knew the note left no room for discussion. It was an order. She had no choice but to go.

One hour later, Kelly arrived at school. She walked down the long empty hall until she saw the sign— *Principal's Office, Mr. Garcia.* As her hand reached for the door, it crashed open. SWOOSH! Jake bolted through.

Kelly jumped out of Jake's way. Palo called from inside, "So, how'd it go?"

"It didn't!" Jake hissed angrily. "I thought this was supposed to be a democracy. We live in America. You're supposed to have a voice. Ha! Guess Garcia never heard of that!"

Imitating Mr. Garcia, Jake said in a whiny voice, "Dolphin Dives is a great program. It will be good for you. A great way to spend your summer."

Kelly slipped around Jake and into the waiting room. She noticed Tyler sitting next to Palo.

"I'll get out of this somehow," Jake's angry voice echoed down the hall.

Kelly knew Jake was bossed around by his brother. And now the school was telling him what to do too. She worried that if they told him what to do with the dolphins, it just might be too much.

"Hey!" Jake's cry came from down the hallway. "Can't you keep that stupid chair out of my way?"

A few seconds later, they heard Betsy struggling to open the door. Palo rushed to hold the door for her. The color had drained from her face. "He hurt his ankle," she muttered.

"He'll live," Palo said after making sure Jake was out of earshot.

Kelly watched the color rise in Betsy's face. Then Kelly noticed Betsy taking long, calming breaths. We must have read the same article, Kelly decided.

Kelly was sure that Betsy was as afraid as she was. But Betsy covered it up by yelling. Just the opposite of me, Kelly thought.

Then Betsy turned to Palo and asked, "What's with Jake?"

"He just came out of Garcia's office. He tried to get out of Dolphin Dives."

"His plan didn't work," Betsy sniffed. "But mine will. I'm not going in the water."

Palo was called into the office. A few minutes later, the door flew open again. Palo danced out of Mr. Garcia's office singing, "Yes. Yes. I'm alive. I'm going swimming at Dolphin Dives."

Palo grinned and waved to the others. His feet danced down the hall.

"Well, at least one person's happy," Tyler said. "But I'm sure to get out of this. My track coach is calling Garcia. I don't have time to play."

Too bad, Kelly thought. He might enjoy it. And I might enjoy getting to know him better.

But after a couple of minutes, Tyler came out of Mr. Garcia's office. He shook his head in disbelief.

"Mr. Garcia thinks I need to 'broaden my horizons,' " Tyler explained to the girls. "He says there's more to life than sports. But I don't know about that," Tyler grumbled.

As he opened the hall door to leave, he said, "See you girls Monday."

"We'll see about that!" Betsy bellowed. But she looked worried. Then she whispered, "If Jake and Tyler couldn't get out of it, I think I have a problem."

But Betsy sat taller and pushed past Kelly. She entered the principal's office and flipped the door closed behind her. Betsy's case would be different, Kelly thought. Betsy had a real reason not to go.

Kelly sat alone. She reached into her pocket and pulled out the book *Island of the Blue Dolphins*. She flipped through the pages. She was too nervous to actually read.

Five minutes passed. After another ten minutes, Betsy came out. Tears streamed down her face. Kelly stood and placed a hand on Betsy's shoulder.

Betsy reached up and angrily threw off Kelly's hand. "I don't want your pity," she sobbed. "I just don't want to go back. Taking people out of wheelchairs and throwing them in the water with killer beasts isn't right. It's not fair!"

Kelly wanted to tell Betsy that dolphins weren't killers. They had actually saved human lives. But Kelly couldn't speak—and Betsy wouldn't listen.

Betsy left. Her wheels burned a path behind her.

Then a voice from behind the door called, "Kelly? Are you there?"

Kelly forced herself up. Her legs swayed like seawater. She straightened her back. Chin held high, she marched into Mr. Garcia's office.

"Do you have anything you want to say?" he asked.

Kelly shook her head.

"You don't want to complain about the Dolphin Dives program?" he asked.

Her eyes were wide with fear. Her lips quivered. But she shook her head again.

Mr. Garcia understood. He walked around his desk and perched on the edge. "I'm sorry, Kelly. I know you don't speak, but I had to try. We really want to help you."

Mr. Garcia looked at Kelly kindly. "Somehow we think this new program may hold the answer. You won't have to do anything you don't want to. Think of it as an adventure. We're hoping you'll all be pleasantly surprised. Kids come from all over the world to be with the dolphins. You have them in your own backyard. And who knows, you may even like it."

Mr. Garcia stepped forward and extended his hand to Kelly. She stood and put her clammy hand in his. He smiled warmly and added, "Good luck."

Kelly forced a smile. I'll need more than luck, she thought.

Leaving the school, Kelly saw Betsy waiting for her ride. Kelly walked over and handed Betsy the dolphin book she'd brought from home.

"Thanks," Betsy muttered, looking surprised. "I love this book. Are you sure you're finished with it?"

Kelly nodded just as Betsy's van drove up. Kelly waved and walked away.

Betsy lowered the window and called out, "Hey, Kelly. Thanks for the book. See you Monday."

A grin played on Kelly's face as she waved. Suddenly, Monday didn't seem so bad.

6

Testing the Waters

Monday arrived quickly. Kelly climbed on the bus and heard the doors close. She looked around. Everyone was there, but no one was speaking.

Kelly slid into the front seat. With a bounce and a choking roar, the old yellow bus began the trip to Kove Key. At first, the busy streets were lined with buildings and houses. Then they passed long stretches of open flatlands.

They passed Homestead. It was a community that had been devastated years ago by Hurricane Andrew. A few houses were still piles of rubble. Kelly thought about how awful it would be to lose your home, your belongings—and even members of your family. But then, she knew how horrible that was.

At first, Kelly had loved their new home in Florida. It had been fun decorating her room. Mom had made new lavender curtains. And she and Dad had picked out the wallpaper. She'd even helped him hang it.

It was the last thing they had done together. Now she wanted to rip the paper off the walls.

She'd never forget that day. It had been three years ago this month.

It was her fault. It had been her words that had killed her dad. She was the one who had asked for the wallpaper. Maybe if they'd just painted like Dad had suggested, he wouldn't have fallen off the ladder and died.

The doctor said it had been a heart attack. Dad had suffered the attack and then fallen. There was nothing anyone could have done.

But Kelly knew it was her fault. They should have

painted. But Dad had said, "Anything for my Princess Flaming Hair."

That's what he'd called her. Tears flooded Kelly's eyes. She forced her eyes shut. She'd give anything to hear him say those words once more.

In one day, her world had crumbled. It was like a puzzle that had scattered into a thousand pieces. And when the pieces were finally put back together, there was one missing. Now the puzzle wasn't the same without it. There was a hole no one else could fill.

Her mom tried, but she was dealing with her own grief. Kelly could see the tears her mom tried to hide. So Kelly hid her tears too.

But every night, Kelly cried herself to sleep. Tears soaked her pillow. But they were silent tears—and silent cries for help. So no one would know. And her words would never hurt anyone again.

Yet the rest of the world went on around her. Kelly wondered how people could just go on shopping and talking and playing and laughing. The world hadn't stopped for Kelly's pain.

"Kelly, are you okay?" Betsy asked.

Embarrassed, Kelly wiped the backs of her hands across her face. She nodded.

Misunderstanding the tears, Betsy touched Kelly's hand. "I know. I'm scared too. I read your dolphin book again. And I watched dolphin videos. But I'm still scared."

Kelly smiled. It was nice to have a friend—someone who shared her fears.

"Okay, we're here," Tyler announced enthusiastically. He looked like someone ready to start a new race.

I guess he's accepted Dolphin Dives, Kelly thought. She liked how he put his whole self into whatever he did—whether it was running or swimming with dolphins.

Would she ever be that excited about anything again? she wondered. But seeing Tyler's excitement made Kelly feel better.

Palo bounced off the bus. He was happy as usual.

The lift moved Betsy. She muttered, "Well, I'm glad *they're* happy."

"Come on, Betsy. I'll help you cool off," Jake snarled. He grabbed Betsy's chair and ran toward the dock.

"Hey!" Betsy screamed. She looked panicked. "Help me!" she yelled, looking toward Kelly.

Kelly grabbed her throat. Jake wouldn't actually throw Betsy in, would he? She raced after them.

It was Tyler who actually stopped Jake. Tyler grabbed a chair handle and pulled them to a stop.

"Not funny." Tyler glared at Jake. Daggers flew between them.

"Not funny," Jake mimicked, giving Tyler a shove. "Such a hero!"

Betsy gasped. The wheelchair shook as Tyler jerked back from Jake's touch.

But Tyler turned away from Jake. He knew Jake was looking for a fight. That would get him kicked out of the program.

Tyler carefully pushed Betsy into the shade near the table. Kelly joined them. As she approached the table, two dolphin fins surfaced.

Betsy asked, "I wonder if it's good for dolphins to be captives?" Betsy squeezed her chair. She knew how they felt.

"Yeah. They're locked up like prisoners," Jake added. "It's cruelty to animals. Haven't you heard about protecting animals? It's mean to lock them up."

Kelly looked at Jake's face. He was serious. But was he concerned for the dolphins—or for himself? Kelly thought about Jake's home life. Was he locked up at home? And who protected *him*?

"Good for you, Jake," Sue said, joining the group. "I'm glad you're thinking about the dolphins. Their safety is a top priority here. Let me tell you how they came here."

"Did you catch them?" Palo asked seriously.

"No," Sue replied. "We *never* capture dolphins. We've rescued a few that have been injured or sick. But when they were well, we let them go."

"So how do you get them?" Palo asked.

"Some of our dolphins have been in shows and wouldn't survive living in the ocean. So they're retired here," Sue explained.

"My grandfather retired to Florida," Tyler said. "Just like the dolphins."

Sue smiled and continued. "A few dolphins were born here."

"But they're not free," Jake hissed. "They're trapped." Jake wasn't giving up.

"Many could be free if they chose to be. In fact, sometimes we give them their freedom. When big storms or hurricanes come, we let the dolphins swim free for their own safety."

"So how come they don't swim away?" Betsy asked.

"They like it here," Sue said. "We love them, and they love us. We feed and care for them. They don't have to perform to eat. They jump and play because they want to."

As if on cue, two shiny blue-gray dolphins arched out of the water.

"There they go again," Palo said.

"I've been reading about dolphins," Tyler said. "One book said they could recognize their mothers even after being separated for years."

"That's true, Tyler," Sue said. "Dolphins make sounds at different pitches. The mother gives her young a special call. Just like your mother gave you a name. That's how dolphins know their own."

"That's cool," Betsy said.

"Dolphins are smart," Sue added. "Maybe someday we'll be smart enough to understand all they have to teach us."

"That's stupid," Jake mumbled. "They're just dumb fish."

"Mammals," Sue corrected. "Now, get your gear. It's time to swim!"

Another dolphin appeared and tail-walked near them.

"Look, Dreamer's inviting you in," Sue said.

Palo shouted, "I'm ready!"

"Me too," Tyler said, adjusting his goggles.

"Dreamer?" Betsy questioned. "How can you tell them apart?"

"Every dolphin is different. Just like humans. Some have markings on their bodies or notches on their fins. Some are teasers. Some like to show off."

Sue handed the boys long barbell floats. "When you first go into the water, you have to hold these."

"But I can swim," Tyler said. He thrust the float back to Sue.

"Me too," Palo protested.

"That's not the point," Sue explained. "If you move your arms, the dolphins might think you're aggressive. They'll stay away. But if your hands are on the float, the dolphins will come close. They'll swim by your side. Or maybe over the back of your legs."

Kelly held her breath. She could almost feel the wet dolphin sliding over her skin.

Then Palo asked, "Can you kick your feet?"

"Sure," Sue said. "Dolphins have flippers, so kicking won't bother them."

"Okay, Tyler and Palo look ready." Sue looked around. "Anyone else want to try?"

Jake snapped, "Not me."

Kelly watched Jake. He looked ready to pounce. He had scared Betsy earlier. What else would he do? Jake could be dangerous. But if he tried something, what would she do? Kelly wondered.

"Not me. Never." Betsy moved farther away from the water.

"Kelly, do you want to try?" Sue asked.

Kelly knew she wasn't ready. She shook her head. Besides, she had to watch Jake.

"Well, come and sit on the floating dock," Sue invited.

Kelly didn't want to. But she did want to watch the guys with the dolphins. And she could still keep an eye on Jake from the dock.

She saw Jake hidden in the shadows. Kelly felt a creepy chill as she climbed down to the floating dock.

Kelly sat on the dock with her feet dangling in the cool water. She watched Tyler and Palo float by. The water looked black. Kelly wondered if they could see any dolphins.

Suddenly, Kelly gasped. Her eyes widened. Frozen, she watched her foot move up out of the water. It was resting on a dolphin's nose!

She stared at the huge dark eye only an arm's length away. The cold, velvety nose tickled the bottom of her foot. Then a warm, peaceful current filled her.

Kelly spotted Jake. He was watching her. She could swear he almost smiled. Realizing she had noticed him, Jake turned away. Kelly hoped her dolphin moment had affected Jake too.

Kelly returned her attention to Dreamer. He balanced Kelly's foot on the end of his nose while sliding down in the water. Kelly's foot floated. Then Dreamer lifted it again.

Kelly was in love. Dreamer's grin filled her. Kelly's worries floated away. She and Dreamer were friends. Up went one foot, then the other.

When Dreamer disappeared, Kelly's heart sank. But then in a flash, he was back. He swam closer this time. Now eyeball to eyeball, Kelly and Dreamer communicated without words.

Worlds of understanding passed between them. *All will be okay*, Dreamer seemed to say. *Things won't be the same as they were. But they will be good.* A calm filled Kelly. The future looked brighter.

Dreamer opened his mouth wide. "Kelly," Sue instructed. "Pet his tongue."

TOP FIN: DOLPHIN DIVES

Kelly looked at Dreamer again. She noticed there were a lot of teeth around that tongue. But she gathered her courage and reached into Dreamer's mouth.

Her hand rested on his tongue. Her fingertips tingled on the wet pink surface. She moved her hand slowly. The tongue felt like a curved ski slope sprinkled with sand.

Dreamer's eyes laughed. He liked this. Kelly shivered as she felt each tiny bump on Dreamer's tongue.

Sue interrupted the moment. "Tyler, Nicky wants to dive," she called. "Leave your float and go!"

Hearing Sue's voice, Dreamer disappeared under the water. Kelly turned her gaze to Tyler.

Tyler's long body was dwarfed by the 500-pound dolphin at his side. Tyler dove under. In an instant, Nicky dove with him. His tail fluke sent sprays of water high into the air. Tyler came up and then dove again. Nicky followed every move.

"Palo!" Sue yelled from the side. "Splash wants to give you a ride. See, she's rolling onto her side. Let go of the float and grab her dorsal fin."

Palo looked confused.

"The top fin," Sue explained.

Palo nodded in understanding. His eyes danced as he prepared to ride with Splash. He put his hand out, thumb down. Splash swam into it.

"Hold on!" Sue shouted.

Kelly watched Palo zoom past. They left a white wake. They moved faster and faster. Kelly's eyes followed Palo and Splash racing by.

Kelly pulled her feet onto the dock. She wrapped her arms tightly around her legs. She shivered in the hot Florida sun. This was getting scary—and also a bit thrilling, she had to admit.

After a few minutes, Sue called, "Palo. Tyler. Link arms and swim. Kick hard."

They did. Then they spit out their snorkels and laughed. Splash and Nicky raced back and forth in front of them.

"I've seen that," Betsy said. "That's how dolphins surf waves in front of boats."

"It's called 'riding the wake,' " Sue said. "For dolphins, it's like a carnival ride."

Just then, a fourth dolphin appeared and squirted a huge spray over Jake and Betsy by the table. Sue laughed as they wiped salty water from their faces. Jake and Betsy weren't laughing.

"Oh, by the way," Sue said, "meet Squirt!"

"Very funny," Betsy protested. But she didn't really sound angry this time.

But Jake was quick to react in anger. Glaring, he kicked stones at Squirt.

Sue raced over. She grabbed Jake's shoulders and spoke furiously. "Don't you ever do that again! No one hurts the dolphins! Human beings are dolphins' biggest threat. But we promise to protect them here. Do you understand?"

"Hey, man," Jake growled, knocking Sue's hands off. "Cool it! You're losing it."

Disgusted, Sue turned away from Jake. She blew the whistle to call the boys out of the water.

Everyone listened as Palo and Tyler raved about their swim.

"Hey, mon, that was the coolest ever. They're so soft—like silk," Palo sighed.

Tyler joined in. "More like wet glass. Smooth but with strong, hard muscles."

Kelly knew what they were talking about. She remembered Dreamer's smooth, wet touch tickling her foot.

But Kelly was concerned about Jake. He wasn't happy. His eyes had become thin slits as they roamed over the water. Kelly felt sweat slide down her back. What would he do next?

He snarled as Palo and Tyler talked. Kelly wondered if Sue or Betsy sensed Jake's rage. But they were too busy listening to Palo and Tyler.

But Jake wasn't paying attention to them. His eyes darted over the water. Was Jake planning something? Kelly worried. Should she let the others know?

But, as usual, she kept quiet.

7

One with
the Dolphins

On the ride home, Palo couldn't keep quiet. "Hey, mon. You have to do it. It's like flying. Like you're a bird. You're a fish. You're free. You're one with the dolphin."

"Dolphins aren't fish. They're mammals," Betsy pointed out. She might not admit it, but she had been paying attention.

Then Betsy asked, "Weren't you scared, Palo?"

"No, mon." Palo moved closer to Betsy. He spoke softly, "You have to try it. When Splash looked at me, it was like we were friends forever. She liked me. Just as I am. And you know how I am. I goof around. I trip. I fall. I get in trouble a lot. But Splash didn't care. She liked me. And I knew she wouldn't hurt me."

"What . . . what did she feel like?" Betsy asked.

"Glass. Wet glass. Smooth. Your hand just glides along her skin. But she's solid as a rock. There's power in her muscles. Great strength."

Kelly listened, remembering Dreamer's velvety touch on her foot.

Tyler asked Palo, "What was the best thing about your ride?"

"The best thing for me was feeling graceful. And feeling like I was part of a team. You probably won't understand this. I mean, you're a great athlete. Everyone always wants you on their team. But not me. I'm clumsy. I drop things and fall over things. You don't know what it's like to always be picked last."

Kelly saw the look Betsy gave Palo. Betsy, too, knew the pain of feeling left out—of being different. No one picked her first, either.

"Sorry," Palo swallowed. He winked at Betsy in understanding.

Then he continued, "When I was in the water with Splash, it was like we were one. I was cool. Coordinated. Riding smoothly. I was as powerful as the dolphin. I felt as if I could do anything. And you know what? Maybe I can."

"Ha!" Jake snorted from the back of the bus. But he'd been listening too.

Kelly looked at Jake. She could see that he was still angry. She shook off a chill and turned her attention to Tyler.

"Well, I'm definitely riding a dolphin next week," Tyler said. "Diving with Nicky was fun. But riding him would be better."

Kelly watched as Tyler spoke about his swim. Maybe Dolphin Dives was working. Tyler was interested in something besides track. And Palo had gained confidence.

Then Tyler surprised Kelly by moving into the empty seat next to her. Everyone on the bus grew quiet. They were lost in their own thoughts.

Kelly glanced shyly at Tyler. Her face flushed. She nervously grabbed a curl, wrapped it around her finger, and chewed on the end.

No! She commanded herself. She dropped the curl. Grow up! she told herself. She tried to take a calming breath, but it came in spurts. Tyler was so close.

"Kelly," he whispered. "I saw you with Dreamer. You really have to try going in. You'll love it. I know you will."

Kelly blinked at Tyler. Was she dreaming? He had paid attention to her. And he cared. Why?

Their eyes met. Hers widened. His eyes were the same turquoise blue as the waters around the keys. And they were warm. They reminded her of smiling pools.

Let me drown in them, Kelly thought. She smiled back. Tyler's eyes expressed understanding—and friendship.

Tyler leaned closer and whispered, "I have to tell you something, Kelly."

She felt his breath move into her ear. She melted.

His voice lowered. "Something happened today. I didn't tell anyone else. But once, when I dove under the water, I turned over on to my back. I had a dolphin's-eye view of the world.

"The sun pushed through the water like golden rods. But I could see through them. And Nicky swam through those gold rays. Light scattered and sparkled everywhere. Then Nicky stopped. He just floated there. A beautiful dark dolphin silhouetted between the sun and me." Tyler closed his eyes, seeing it again.

Silence filled the space between Tyler and Kelly. But it wasn't a wall of silence. It was a bridge—a magical silence.

Kelly nodded. From his description, Kelly could picture what he had seen under the water. She could imagine the beauty and the wonder. She rested her head against the seat and breathed deeply.

Yes, she decided. She was ready. Next time she would do it. Next week, she would swim with the dolphins.

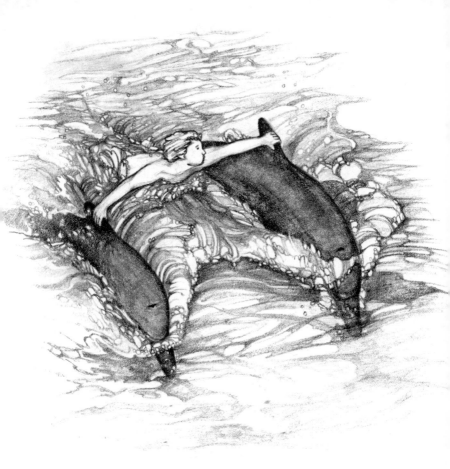

8

Seeing Without Eyes

The bus bounced along the highway. It was on its way to the third session of Dolphin Dives.

Kelly had promised herself she'd swim today. But now, in the salty air, she shook like a jellyfish.

Everyone was quiet. Palo and Tyler slept. Betsy read. The summer heat hung like a heavy blanket over everyone.

Then Kelly spotted the lump on Jake's head. It was the size of a baseball. His left eye was shut and swam in a sea of purple and black.

He must have been in another fight, Kelly thought. Did his brother hit him? Or someone else? She couldn't even imagine how tough Jake's home life must be. But the bruised eye made her wince.

Jake caught her staring at him. His good eye stared back. He shot her a look that could freeze water.

But Kelly faced him. *Take your anger out on me*, she ordered silently. *Leave the dolphins alone*.

Screeching brakes shattered the quiet. They had reached Kove Key.

Betsy's shrill voice woke everyone. "I still can't believe they're making us do this! Throwing kids in with killer creatures is crazy. It's instant death."

Waking up, Palo tried to calm her. "Oh, Betsy, they're gentle as guppies."

"Gentle? Ha! They weigh hundreds of pounds. How could they be gentle?"

"You'll see. I can't explain it," Palo said. "But once you ride with a dolphin, you won't want to stop. I can't wait to ride again!"

"But I want to ride Splash today," Tyler said. "Last week, she stuck to you like a magnet."

"Hey, mon, I can't help it. I'm just lovable." Palo laughed.

"Hey, guys, listen," Betsy called from her book. "Dolphins have sonar. It's like radar. They see without their eyes. They see using sound waves."

"How can you see sound?" Palo asked.

Betsy explained, "The sonar goes out and bounces off a fish and returns. That's called *echolocation*. Now the dolphin knows exactly where the fish is. Then the dolphin can capture its dinner easily."

"Cool!" Palo said. "Do any other animals have sonar?"

"I don't know. Let's ask Sue," Betsy suggested.

Kelly climbed off the bus. The fence loomed ahead, both familiar and frightening.

As the group entered, Splash, Dreamer, Nicky, and Squirt jumped and dove. Splash sent a wall of water over the dock. But the kids stayed clear this time.

Kelly held back as she watched the others pick through the gear.

Then Betsy asked Sue, "I read about dolphin sonar. Do other animals have sonar?"

"Bats do," Sue answered. "And they're kind of funny. They locate bugs and then change their pitch as they close in. They use their wings to bat bugs into their mouth."

"*Bat* them! I get it," Palo laughed.

Sue smiled. "I read once that dolphins saved shipwrecked sailors using their sonar. The dolphins 'saw' the sailors in storms and gave them rides or pushed them to shore."

"Like I rode Splash," Palo added.

"True," Sue agreed. "And once a really strange thing happened here."

The kids inched closer—even Jake. "Once a woman noticed that the dolphins were swimming under her instead of by her side. Later she wrote saying she was having a baby. She said the dolphins used their sonar and saw the baby before she even knew she was pregnant."

Palo whistled. "My mom had a regular sonogram at the doctor's office. But that lady had a dolphin sonogram!"

"No way!" Betsy cried. "That didn't happen."

"It's true," Sue said. "And when people have body parts that don't work, the dolphins know. They go right to that part and try to help it."

Betsy's face paled. "Could they help me?"

Sue answered, "I don't know, Betsy. But I do know that I have worked with others who felt that the dolphins helped them. And they loved being with the dolphins."

"How did they help those people?" Betsy asked.

"Once a boy who didn't speak much put his first two words together," Sue said.

"What did he say?" Betsy asked. She didn't notice Kelly's face turning red.

"Out now!" Sue answered, smiling.

"In now!" Palo cried, biting the snorkel. Geared up, he walked to the dock.

The kids scattered. Betsy sat under the umbrella. She wasn't rushing into anything.

Kelly climbed to the floating dock. She dangled her feet in the cool water. She thought about the boy speaking his first words. It had been so long since she had talked. Could she even speak anymore?

Palo and Tyler swam with the dolphins.

"Boys," Sue called to them. "Hold this hula hoop under the water. The dolphins will use their sonar to swim through it. Listen for their sonar clicks."

Squirt was the first one through.

Palo cried, "Cool! It sounds like electricity."

"That's right." Sue grinned.

"Electricity? In the water? That could kill you," Betsy said.

"No," Sue explained. "It sounds like electricity, but it's the sonar sound waves."

Kelly wondered about sonar. Was seeing without eyes like speaking without words? Kelly knew it was possible to communicate without speaking. And she often knew what others were thinking, even when they weren't talking.

"Wow!" Betsy squealed suddenly. "Did you see that? Squirt jumped over Palo and Tyler."

Kelly and Betsy clapped. Rainbow balloons sprinkled the air.

Then Betsy pointed. "Look, there's Jake."

Kelly knew he must have used the side ladder. He didn't have flippers on. He was kicking furiously. Water splashed all around him.

Sue's face flushed in anger. "Jake, here!" she shouted, throwing him a barbell float.

He shook his head in defiance and swam away. He splashed wildly.

"Take the float or get out," Sue ordered. "You're upsetting the dolphins."

Hurling himself at the float, Jake grabbed it. But he kicked even harder.

Sue turned to Tyler. "Okay, Tyler. Ready for a ride?"

Tyler nodded. He could see Nicky and Squirt on either side of him. He stretched both arms out. He clasped his hands around the top fins. His thumbs pointed down.

They whizzed by faster than any human could swim. Kelly applauded.

Dreamer came over and nudged Kelly's leg. Kelly pet Dreamer's sleek nose.

Sue's whistle cut the moment short. Kelly couldn't believe the hour was over. Tyler and Palo climbed out. But Jake stayed in. Sue whistled again, harder this time.

Jake swam to the middle of the pool. He looked around, enraged.

Kelly realized what was happening. Not one dolphin would go near Jake. And he was furious. He was rejected at home and at school. Now even the dolphins left him alone.

Finally, Jake climbed onto the dock. Water gushed off him. He threw his equipment down like grenades.

"Stupid animals," Jake spit through clenched teeth.

In a calm voice, Sue asked, "Jake, why do you think they didn't come to you?"

" 'Cause they're stupid," Jake sneered. "They didn't even know I was there."

"They knew," Betsy chimed in. "Because of their sonar."

Jake whipped around and glared at Betsy.

Sue interrupted. "Jake, what is it that dolphins like to do most?"

"Play," Palo piped in, trying to help.

"Right, Palo. They love to play," Sue agreed.

As if on cue, three dolphins jumped and dove. Everyone but Jake enjoyed the grand finale.

Sue pressed on. "Jake, do you think the dolphins knew you wanted to play?"

"I kept telling them to come, the stupid beasts." Jake glared toward the water.

"Maybe you can't tell dolphins what to do," Sue suggested. "Dolphins do what they want. I wonder what would happen if you acted like you wanted to play instead of giving orders?"

"Well, don't worry about that," Jake sputtered. He shook his dripping hair. Water flew everywhere. "I'm not swimming with fish again."

"Mammals," Betsy whispered. "And more like us than we know."

"Maybe they're like you, fish face," Jake said, pushing Betsy aside. "But not like me." He charged toward the gate, scattering stones along the way.

The rest of them stored their gear and headed to the bus. Jake sat alone. Kelly saw that he was like a volcano ready to erupt. Kelly wondered if Jake *ever* played. Maybe he didn't know how.

"Hi," Tyler said, sitting next to her. Kelly blinked in surprise.

"Next week," he said. He placed his hand over hers on the seat. "Next week you'll go in."

He put his head back. In a minute, he was asleep. Kelly didn't move. His hand rested on hers. It felt like fire. Warmth spread through her body. She wanted this ride to last forever.

9

Shakespeare

For Kelly, the week between each dolphin dive flew by. She didn't even worry about summer passing too quickly.

Soon, school would start again. Kelly smiled at the thought. She'd see Tyler every day then.

Kelly couldn't sit still. She'd made a decision. Today she would go in the water with the dolphins. She was still scared. But she would do it anyway.

"Shut up!" Jake ordered Tyler and Palo. The two boys had been talking in the back of the bus.

Oh, no, Kelly thought. Trouble.

Tyler and Palo lowered their voices. They didn't want a brawl. But they weren't taking orders from Jake, either. They continued to talk in hushed voices.

At Dolphin Dives, Palo and Tyler geared up right away. Kelly watched Palo clumsily land with a bang on the floating dock. Ripples spread out across the water. But once Palo entered the water, he was a natural. He was almost as graceful as the dolphins.

Tyler joined Palo. Tyler swam as well as he did everything else. Kelly watched for a few minutes. Then she knelt on the dock.

"Are you going in?" Betsy asked.

Kelly's eyes met Betsy's. Kelly nodded. Betsy gave her a thumbs-up. "Go for it."

Then Betsy asked Sue, "What's up? The dolphins are ignoring us."

Sue smiled, "Good observation, Betsy. See how half of the deck is roped off. We had a special event yesterday. Juliet gave birth."

"A baby dolphin!" Betsy shouted. She used her arms to raise herself up and look. Kelly stood up.

"No, girls. Not yet. Baby dolphins have a hard time surviving in captivity. Juliet lost one last year. Second births have a better chance. But we don't want to make Juliet nervous."

"Sorry," Betsy whispered, settling back in her seat.

Palo and Tyler had heard everything. Tyler took his snorkel out and spoke softly, "We were wondering why our pals weren't playing. Can we look through the fence?"

"Yes," Sue said. "You're in the water, so you're like one of them. You girls can look from the deck."

"I think I see the baby," Betsy whispered. "It's nursing."

A hush fell. Juliet and her baby floated by. Juliet's large eyes invited them to admire.

"How much does the baby weigh?" Betsy asked quietly.

"About 40 pounds. It's really too early to weigh him. But he appears healthy," Sue replied.

"Who's the father?" Jake demanded. "Is he caged too? Just like the kid?"

Kelly understood Jake's rage. She knew Jake's dad wasn't home much and his mom had left after Jake was born. His brothers had blamed Jake. They said he cried so much that she couldn't stand it anymore. So his brothers had locked him in a closet.

That's what Kelly had heard anyway. And she believed it.

Now, Jake didn't like being closed in. And he didn't cry anymore.

"I know," Betsy said. "If the mother is Juliet, the father must be Romeo."

Sue laughed. "Good for you, Betsy. You know your literature. Romeo is our biggest dolphin. He weighs over 700 pounds."

Hearing that, Tyler asked, "Where is he? Can I swim with the giant?"

"He's across the channel," Sue said. "Romeo is big, but gentle. We use him with folks in our floating chair."

Betsy choked, "You use the *biggest* dolphin for people in chairs? That's too weird." Then she quickly changed the subject. "What's the baby's name?"

"We don't have one yet," Sue said. "Do you have any suggestions?"

"Yes," Betsy's face brightened. "With a mother named Juliet and a father named Romeo, the baby should be Shakespeare!"

Sue laughed. "Great idea, Betsy. I'll suggest it."

"What was it like when Shakespeare was born?" Tyler asked.

Exactly what I was wondering, Kelly thought. Thanks, Tyler. Sometimes Kelly grew tired of having to wait for other people to ask her questions.

"Good question," Sue said. "Well, when we knew she was about to deliver, we closed the place. Then all the dolphins grew quiet. They just waited."

"They knew," Betsy said confidently. "They used their sonar."

"You're probably right," Sue agreed. "Finally, the baby was born. After the birth, you should have seen this place. It was like a circus. There were dolphins jumping, clicking, and flipping all over."

"Cool," Palo said. "It was a celebration."

The group spread out again. Tyler and Palo swam. Kelly sat on the dock. Betsy sat nearby.

Dreamer came and nudged Kelly's foot. Kelly lifted her feet and put on flippers. She adjusted the mask and bit on the snorkel. Breathe, she told herself. In. Out.

Slowly, Kelly lowered herself into the water. She felt the cool water surround her body.

Betsy pointed at Kelly. "Sue, look!" she said.

Sue nodded.

Kelly stretched out. She felt at home in the water. She floated facedown. Her white knuckles curled around a float. She barely moved her legs up and down.

Kelly felt the salty sea fill her ears and muffle all sounds. Her long hair fanned out around her.

Then Nicky appeared. Excitement bubbled inside of Kelly. But she felt no fear.

Other dolphins swam by. Soon, Splash swam on her right and Squirt on her left. Then Squirt was pushed away. Dreamer took over. Splash swam away.

Kelly swam eyeball to eyeball with Dreamer. A peace rolled through her. She and Dreamer were communicating. They didn't need words. Her heart raced with joy. She'd remember this moment forever.

Suddenly, a loud, piercing whistle interrupted Kelly's peaceful swim.

"Time to leave," Sue called.

"But we just got in!" Palo protested.

"It just seems that way," Sue said. "Time's up."

"No rides today," Palo said, hauling himself out of the water. He looked disappointed as salty puddles surrounded his feet.

"The dolphins knew it would be too much for Juliet and Shakespeare. Next week they'll be playful again," Sue said.

After boarding the bus, Kelly sat close to the window. She left room, just in case Tyler wanted to join her. She closed her eyes, remembering her swim.

Then Kelly sensed she wasn't alone. Her eyes popped open. She found herself eye to eye with Jake. He was sitting in the seat across from her.

The bus started. Kelly bolted upright. Jake's stormy eyes bore into hers.

She read his thoughts. *You think you're special— swimming with the dolphins. Just wait. I'll show you how tough they really are.*

10

Swimming with Romeo

Another week passed. Kelly felt like it had dragged. She was excited to return to Dolphin Dives. It was their fifth session—only one more left. Kelly tried not to think about that.

Her nerves felt like electric currents. Every bump in the road sent shocks through her. She wanted to swim, but she couldn't forget Jake's silent warning.

What was he going to do? Kelly was sure he'd try something. She worried for the dolphins. And she feared for the baby.

"You seem nervous," Betsy said. "Are you okay?"

Kelly nodded. If only I could tell her, she thought. But even if I wrote it down, I don't have proof. So she alone would have to stop him.

Betsy patted Kelly's shoulder, misunderstanding her nervousness. "You did fine in the water." Then Betsy added, "Maybe *I'll* even try today."

Sweat beaded on Betsy's brow. Kelly squeezed Betsy's hand in encouragement.

The rest of the trip passed in silence. Green grasses waved against white sand. Salty air filled the bus.

They arrived and rushed inside.

"How are Juliet and Shakespeare?" Betsy asked.

Sue smiled. "They're fine. And, Betsy, the baby is now officially named Shakespeare."

"Cool," Betsy said.

"Hey, Sue," Palo said. "Like, mon, I'm getting used to this. I love swimming with dolphins. And next week is our last. Can we keep coming after that?"

"Can we?" Tyler seconded the question.

Kelly stared at Tyler in surprise. She thought he'd want to get back to his running.

"Great minds do think alike," Sue said. "Last week, *I* asked if we could continue."

Kelly was surprised to hear this. In the beginning, Sue had been nervous about working with this group. Now she was asking for them to stay.

"And . . ." Tyler prompted, waiting for the answer.

"The school said maybe they'd run the program in the fall. It could be an after-school program."

Palo sang, "Dolphin Dives, mon, it's so cool. We'll go swimming after school."

But Jake stopped the song and laughter by kicking stones. They pinged like shots against the metal shed. "No way," he mumbled.

Kelly turned. The others did too. But then they looked away. It wasn't worth it. They ignored Jake and began gearing up. Jake hid himself in the shadows.

Betsy climbed into the aqua chair. Kelly watched Sue strap Betsy in and slip on the water socks. Tyler and Palo swam with their dolphin pals.

Only Kelly paid attention to Jake. She could feel his rage. She didn't want to take her eyes off him. She'd give up her dolphin swim today.

Sue lowered Betsy and the aqua chair into the water.

"It's cold!" Betsy shrieked, gripping the chair. "Help! I'm sinking!"

"You're doing fine," Sue encouraged.

Slowly Betsy's legs disappeared into the blue sea.

The cool water rippled over her knees and thighs. She gasped when a wave brushed against her belly. Her hands were covered by water. She held on tighter.

"Oh . . ." Betsy moaned. Her still legs sank into the sea. Then she yelled, "Hey!"

Betsy's eyes filled with tears as she watched one leg rise up on the nose of a dolphin.

"Look," she whispered. "He moved my leg!"

A tear fell from Kelly's eye.

The leg went back down.

Now Sue encouraged Betsy. "You won't sink. And you're strapped in. Let go of the arms, and run your fingers through the water."

Betsy inhaled. She shut her eyes and let go.

"Good job," Sue said. "Feel the water. It's not that cold. Now open your eyes."

Betsy did. Then she reached a hand out.

"Aaaah," she sighed as Romeo's huge form glided smoothly under her fingertips. Ripples of pleasure coursed through her.

Suddenly a loud cry thundered across the water. "Nooooo!" Kelly shrieked as she dove across the pebbles, throwing herself at Jake.

She hit his hand. Rocks tumbled out of it. They both fell to the ground. Scraped and bleeding, they slid across the sharp stones toward the water where the baby dolphin swam. Blood oozed from gashes and cuts on Kelly's and Jake's bare arms and legs.

Everyone stared at them in shock. No one believed what they were seeing—or what they'd heard!

Kelly didn't know how long she and Jake lay on the stones. Their arms and legs were twisted and bleeding. Seconds seemed like minutes. Time stood still.

Finally, Kelly noticed movement around her. Sue was taking Betsy out of the aqua chair. Water shot behind Palo and Tyler as they soared up the ladder.

"Kelly." Tyler's voice rang like an echo around her head.

But Kelly felt like she was floating above the scene. She was watching it, but she didn't feel as if she were really there.

Tyler reached Kelly first. He pushed Jake aside roughly. Kneeling next to Kelly, he lifted her head up gently. He kept one arm around her shoulder.

"Are you okay? What happened?" Tyler asked.

Kelly pushed herself up on bruised elbows. She shook her head, trying to clear it. Why am I here? Why is everyone staring at me? Then it all came back.

She remembered Jake raising his arm. He was aiming toward the mother and baby dolphin. She couldn't let him hurt them. But she couldn't reach him in time. She had to call out. And . . . she had!

"Kelly," Tyler asked. He used his towel to wipe away blood that was trickling down her arm. "What happened?"

Kelly glanced at Jake. He was crouched like a cornered tiger. But he caught Kelly's eye. Silently he questioned her. *So what are you going to say? That I was going to throw rocks at the baby?*

Their eyes locked. She could read him like a book. If she said anything, it would be over. He would be thrown out of the program—and maybe out of school. Kelly shuddered to think what his family might do to him.

Kelly looked around. What should she do? Tyler was poised like a leopard, ready to attack Jake. She just had to say the word.

Kelly took a deep breath. After all these years of quiet, she refused to let her first words be ones that could hurt. Jake needed a lifeline if he was going to make it. And Kelly knew she had to be the one to throw it.

Kelly stood up. She brushed herself off and sighed, "I slipped."

"What?" Tyler bristled, not believing her for a minute.

Tyler looked from Kelly to Jake. "No way!" he argued. Fire filled his eyes. His hands were fists. Now *he* wanted to fight.

Jake stared at Kelly in disbelief. He knew Kelly understood exactly what he had planned. His mouth hung open. No one had ever stood up for him before—not ever!

Just then, the honking of the bus broke through the silence.

"Oh, no," Palo moaned.

"And next week's our last session," Betsy groaned. "It figures. Now that I like it, it's almost over."

"Hey, Ty," Palo called. "I'll put your gear away."

"Thanks," Tyler called. He helped Kelly toward the bus.

"Kelly, wait. Come here," Sue called. She opened the first aid kit. "This will prevent any infection. And it will stop the bleeding. You too, Jake."

But Jake was gone. He was already on the bus.

The others boarded the bus. Betsy looked at Jake's bleeding arms and legs.

"Are you okay?" she asked.

Jake looked at her, ready to attack. But then he stopped himself. He mumbled, "Yeah, I'm fine."

His eyes darted around. He tried to smile, but he didn't seem to know how. One corner of his mouth curled up awkwardly.

The bus door closed and the motor started to rumble. Sue hollered from outside, "See you next week. I hope to have a surprise for you."

Tyler sat next to Kelly. He muttered, "What could be more of a surprise than Betsy, who's deathly afraid of water, going in the water with dolphins?"

Then he faced Kelly. "Except maybe Miss Kelly,

who never says a word, speaking!" Then he added softly, "Not only does she speak, but she saves a baby dolphin from being stoned."

Shocked, Kelly faced Tyler. How did he know? But she recovered quickly. In a voice as smooth as silk, she murmured, "I slipped." But she couldn't hide the red flush filling her face.

Tyler put his arm around her and said, "And saved another guy's skin!"

Kelly felt the heat of Tyler's fingers through her towel. Her shoulder burned under his touch. She pleaded, "Please don't tell."

"I won't," he promised. They sat in silence for a few moments.

Then Tyler said, "It's good to hear your voice, Kelly. It's soft." His eyes looked over the water at the swaying palm trees. "Like a warm breeze over the gulf."

Kelly smiled and rested her head on his shoulder. His head settled on top of hers. Within minutes, they were both asleep.

11

Rainbow Bridges

The last session arrived before anyone was ready for it. Tyler sat next to Kelly on the bus ride there. They were both quiet.

Kelly wondered if Dolphin Dives would continue. And she wondered if she and Tyler would be part of it. She'd like to continue. But if the group changed, it wouldn't be the same.

She knew that Tyler also liked the swims. But he wanted to get back to running too.

Kelly noticed that Tyler seemed nervous. He kept clasping and unclasping his hands. She hoped he'd tell her what was wrong. When he did, she was shocked.

"Kelly, I was thinking. I bet you'd be good at track. I mean, you have really long legs." Color rushed to his cheeks.

"I mean, I bet you could run fast. I mean . . . I'm saying this all wrong. But have you ever thought about going out for track?"

"N—No," Kelly said, the word stumbling from her mouth. She couldn't believe what she was hearing. He had noticed her legs! "I have good legs?"

"Yeah," he said enthusiastically. "Good. Strong." He turned crimson. Finally he blurted out, "I have to get back to running soon. I thought that maybe you'd like to join me."

Kelly swallowed hard. "Tyler, I can't run like you," she began.

Tyler looked disappointed.

"But I wouldn't mind trying," Kelly continued.

Tyler grinned. "Great! I'll help you. I bet you could make the team. Tryouts are in a few months. I run every morning. Want to join me?"

"I—I could never run with you. You're too good," Kelly stammered.

"Not the whole run," he agreed. "But I had an idea. I run five miles every morning. I pass right by your house. You could join me then. We could circle the lake. That's only about a mile. Want to try?"

He knows where I live, Kelly marveled. Sure, she'd try. She was beginning to feel like she could do anything. "What time would you come by?" she asked.

"Is six o'clock okay? Tomorrow?" he asked.

Six o'clock in the morning? Kelly shuddered. But she'd do anything to spend time with Tyler. Even if it meant getting up at six o'clock in the morning. Actually, Kelly planned in her head, she'd have to get up before six to be ready by six. But that didn't matter . . .

She realized that Tyler was still waiting for an answer. Smiling, she nodded. Then she remembered to speak. "Six o'clock is fine."

She made a mental note—pick up running shoes, buy new shorts, set alarm.

Soon the bumpy ride ended. The door opened, and the kids rushed out. Everyone geared up. Betsy moved to the aqua chair.

"Where's Jake?" Sue asked.

Everyone looked around. Jake wasn't there. When he didn't get on the bus, everyone had assumed his brother would drop him off again.

"I hope he's okay," Betsy worried aloud.

"Believe me," Tyler said. "Jake can take care of himself."

"Let me go make a phone call," Sue said. "Gear up, but don't go in the water."

Kelly was concerned. She really cared about what happened to Jake, she realized in surprise.

Betsy waited by the aqua chair. Palo, Tyler, and Kelly sat on the floating dock.

Finally, Sue returned. "Everything's fine," she told them. "The school said Jake fell off his bike. He broke his arm. He's excused from the program today."

Kelly wondered about the broken arm. Had he really fallen off his bike? She doubted it.

Betsy called, "What about the surprise, Sue?"

"Well . . ." Sue drew out the word. "All right. I'll tell you. Your school has okayed another Dolphin Dives program! Some new kids might join. But all of you have first choice."

"Yahoo!" Palo shouted, throwing his mask in the air. It landed like an orange fish, belly-up in the water.

"Oops! I have to go in and get it," Palo said.

Sue smiled and nodded. Palo slid in. Splash was at his side immediately. The two pals were off.

Tyler slipped into the water too. Like a magnet, Nicky joined him. Tyler pet the wet, rubbery skin.

"Do the dolphins recognize us?" Kelly asked as she pulled on her flippers.

"Sure," Sue said. "Remember, they even know their young after years apart."

"By a sound name," Betsy added. "Do you think Juliet gave Shakespeare a sound name? Kind of like I gave him a name?"

"I'm sure she did," Sue said.

"Do you think dolphins are smarter than humans?" Kelly asked.

"They're smart in different ways," Sue said. "They have sonar and we don't. And I think dolphins have answers to questions we haven't even thought of yet. But we can do things that they can't. We can all learn from one another if we work together."

Just then, Dreamer appeared and gave Kelly's foot a nudge. Kelly laughed. "Hey, not so rough, big guy. I'm coming."

Kelly bit the snorkel and adjusted her mask. She splashed into the cool salty gulf. With her face down, she breathed easily through the snorkel. Holding her arms at her sides, Kelly kicked gently.

She spied Nicky and Dreamer. Kelly relaxed in the water. Time drifted by.

Eventually, Dreamer's nose nudged Kelly's hand. Kelly knew the signal. She reached out. As Dreamer passed, Kelly curled her fingers around Dreamer's top fin.

Lifting her head up, Kelly shared a dolphin's view of where they were going. They soared. She and Dreamer sliced through the water, leaving a white wake behind them. Wind brushed her face. The rush of air dried the misty sprays and left salty kisses.

Whipping through the water, Kelly felt power and joy. She was where she was supposed to be. For the first time in a long time, she felt part of the world around her.

And her dad was part of it too. Somehow, Kelly knew, he was sharing her joy.

Then Dreamer dove beneath the water. Kelly's ride was over.

Kelly removed the snorkel and shouted, "Wow! That was great!"

But Dreamer wasn't finished. Kelly giggled when a dolphin snout nibbled her toes. Her mouth filled with water. She spluttered and exclaimed, "He found my toes!"

"They're smart," Sue smiled. "There are holes in your flippers so your feet can breathe."

"And so dolphins can nibble on your toes," Betsy added playfully.

Sue lowered Betsy into the water. Sue threw in a large red ball. Romeo returned with the ball balanced on his nose. He tossed it to Betsy.

"Yikes," Betsy cried, reaching up and catching it. She tossed it back. The game began.

Tyler swam toward Kelly and removed his snorkel. "Kelly, come and swim with me."

He linked his arm through hers. Their wet hands clasped. Kicking hard, they sped through the water.

Within seconds, Dreamer and Squirt dove and played in the pressure wake in front of them. Golden bubbles reflecting the sunlight filled the air around them. Kelly wanted this moment to last forever.

But then, the moment was shattered. The unwelcome horn from the school bus signaled the end of their last swim.

"Oh, no," Sue protested. "I let time get away from me. Hurry, kids. Out!"

Kelly flopped onto the dock. Tyler joined her. Palo tossed his gear up onto the dock.

"Bye, pals." Palo waved sadly to the dolphins.

Then a small splash caught Kelly's eye. "Hey, little guy, we didn't forget you. Good-bye, Shakespeare," she called, waving.

"Sue, how is Shakespeare doing?" Betsy asked. She sounded as if she owned the dolphin she had named.

"He's doing great," Sue said. "Look!" Shakespeare did a baby flip.

"He's learning fast," Kelly said, laughing.

"And so are you," Sue said, patting Kelly's back. "You have a beautiful voice."

Sue hugged Betsy. "I'm proud of you. It took courage to go back into the water. Can I call you? We're starting a program for kids with special needs. I'd like your help."

"Sure," Betsy replied. She blushed with pride.

Tyler gave Betsy a high five. "Way to go!"

Palo laughed. He gave Betsy and Sue high fives. Then he put on his tunes and danced to the bus.

"Tyler, are you joining us in the fall?" Sue asked.

"I'll check my schedule. I'd like to." He looked serious. "I'll do what I can."

"I understand," Sue said. "And Kelly, how about you?"

"I hope to," Kelly said. "And thanks." Kelly paused. "Will Jake be back?" she asked.

"The school assured me that Jake will be in Dolphin Dives II. He wants to come."

Kelly was glad he'd have another chance. Did Jake really want to come back? Or was the school making him? Either way, Kelly was sure it would be different next time.

Tyler looked at Kelly. "Hey, girl, why are you so

worried about Jake? I'll have to keep an eye on you." He smiled and took her hand as they walked to the bus.

"I just feel bad for Jake," Kelly explained. "He has it rough at home. And I don't think he's quite as tough as he pretends to be."

"Maybe," Tyler admitted. "But I still want him to stay away from you."

With Tyler's warm hand in hers, Kelly wondered if her feet were touching the ground. Kelly couldn't believe the changes—from being invisible to swimming with dolphins. And now, she was holding hands with Tyler.

Sitting on the bus, Tyler asked Kelly, "So, do we have a date? Running tomorrow?"

A date, she thought. That sounds good. Then, with a mischievous grin, she asked, "So, are we swimming this fall?"

He laughed. "We'll see. Do you always answer a question with a question?" Casually, he stretched his arm around Kelly. His fingertips rested gently on her shoulder.

Kelly inched closer, letting her head rest against Tyler's arm. She closed her eyes. She wondered how the dolphins had managed to change them all. Was it the sonar? Or did their joy somehow reach out to people's hearts? Maybe it was what Sue said about having answers to questions we haven't thought of yet.

Warm salty breezes filled the bus. Kelly opened her eyes. The low sun covered the world in liquid amber. She listened to the steady breathing of sleeping kids.

What a group! She thought about Betsy and how she had met the challenge. Kelly wondered if she'd have been that brave after a diving accident.

And then there was Palo. Her grin broadened. He was such a fun guy—a clown on land, but such a natural in the water. He had really became one with the dolphins.

Tyler's arm shifted in his sleep, pulling Kelly closer. The hairs rose on the back of her neck. She sighed. She would never have guessed that the school track star would be interested in her—or that he would have more interests than just running.

Kelly frowned as she thought of Jake. She really hoped he was okay. Maybe her silence had helped him realize that not everyone was out to get him. He had a friend—if he wanted one. And she knew he'd be more successful in the next session of Dolphin Dives.

Finally, Kelly thought about herself. She had found her voice. She didn't have to be invisible anymore. And she'd made friends—real friends.

Just then, her eyes saw a splash far out in the turquoise Atlantic. A gull swooped by the shoreline. She blinked. Then she saw it again. In the distance, a dolphin jumped. Its silvery body glistened, leaving a rainbow bridge that melted into the sea.

"Thank you," she whispered to the dolphins.

Finally, the rolling of the bus and the long day forced Kelly's eyes to close. She fell asleep, dreaming about tomorrow.